HORRO

The 1924 Lorain, Ohio, Tornado

Bonnie Highsmith Taylor

Perfection Learning®

Cover Photo: NOAA
Inside Illustration: Jason Roe
Some images copyright www.arttoday.com.

Dedication

Thanks to Albert C. Doane and the Black River
Historical Society

About the Author

Bonnie Highsmith Taylor is a native Oregonian.
She loves camping in the Oregon mountains and
watching birds and other wildlife. Writing is Ms.
Taylor's first love. But she also enjoys going to
plays and concerts, collecting antique dolls, and
listening to good music.

Ms. Taylor is the author of several Chapter 2
books, including *Terror in the City: The 1906
San Francisco Earthquake* and *Valley of Disaster:
The Johnstown Flood of 1889*. She has also
written novels including *Gypsy in the Cellar* and
Kodi's Mare.

For information, contact
Perfection Learning® Corporation, 1000 North Second Avenue,
P.O. Box 500, Logan, Iowa 51546-0500.
Phone: 1-800-831-4190 • Fax: 1-800-543-2745
perfectionlearning.com
Paperback ISBN 0-7891-5837-x
Cover Craft® ISBN 0-7569-0925-2

TABLE OF CONTENTS

The Path of the 1924 Lorain, Ohio, Tornado

Lake Erie

Tornado path

Sandusky

•Lorain

Chapter 1

"It's not fair," Calvin Moore grumbled. "I have to do everything around here."

HORROR FROM THE SKY

He crammed a huge bite of toast into his mouth. He chewed it angrily. "George doesn't have to do anything," he mumbled.

"Don't talk with your mouth full," Mom said. She began clearing the table.

"Well—" Calvin swallowed. "He doesn't."

"Your brother has a job," Mom said. "You know that. He'll be working all summer."

George had already left for his job at the Steel Stamping Company. Calvin's dad worked there too. He had worked for the company since it had started three years ago.

Mr. Moore had helped his son get the summer job. George would be sweeping floors and picking up scraps of metal.

George was trying to make enough money for a new bicycle. Then he would give his old one to Calvin.

HORROR FROM THE SKY

George had just turned 16. He was a junior in high school.

Calvin's sister, Margie, was 15. She was a sophomore. She had a summer job in a bakery.

Calvin didn't mind Margie having a summer job. She brought home day-old **pastries** nearly every day. Calvin especially liked the cream rolls and ladyfingers. His mom said the whole family would be as fat as pigs by fall.

Most of Margie's chores had been in the house. At least Calvin didn't have to do those. His mother did.

Calvin and George had shared all the outside chores. But now Calvin had to do them alone. He had to clean the chicken **coop** and goat shed. He had to keep all the fences mended. The goats were always tearing them down. He had to clean the rabbit **hutches** and the pigpen.

HORROR FROM THE SKY

When he was done with those chores, Calvin had to feed and water all the animals. He was thankful his mother milked the goats.

Calvin also had to hoe the garden and weed the berries. He had to chop and carry firewood. Even in the summer, firewood was needed for the wood-burning cookstove.

Up until now, it hadn't even seemed like work with George's help. But now, Calvin hated the chores.

He envied George for having a job. Calvin was only 11. It would be several years before he could get a summer job.

School had been out for three weeks, and Calvin had done only one fun thing. He had gone fishing at the lake. And that had been almost two weeks ago.

The Moores lived just outside Lorain, Ohio. The small town was very close to Lake Erie. The family often went to Lakeview Park to picnic, swim, and fish.

After breakfast, Calvin pulled on his boots.

"Clean the chicken coop first," Mom said. "It's really a mess."

Calvin grunted, "Okay."

"And be careful not to disturb the nest boxes," Mom went on. "Two of the hens are **setting**."

Calvin sighed. "Oh, great. That means about 20 more chickens for me to clean up after."

Mrs. Moore laughed. She hugged Calvin. "Poor boy," she said. "You do have a hard life."

That made Calvin feel a little foolish.

"Tell you what," Mom said, still laughing. "Saturday, I'll fry a chicken and make potato salad. Then we'll go to Lakeview Park for a picnic."

HORROR FROM THE SKY

"Saturday is tomorrow!" Calvin shouted. Then he said, "Will you make a chocolate cake too?"

"If you insist," Mom answered.

Calvin ran out the screen door, letting it slam behind him. He skidded to a stop on the porch. "Can I ask Ned to go with us?" he called.

"Yes," Mom answered.

Ned lived in town and was Calvin's best friend. Calvin hadn't seen Ned since vacation began.

Calvin felt a little better. He whistled while he shoveled chicken manure into the wheelbarrow. He even picked up a speckled **pullet** and smoothed her feathers. Calvin was careful not to disturb the two hens in the nest boxes.

When the wheelbarrow was full, Calvin wheeled it to a spot on the far side of the property. Next spring, the dried manure would be used for garden **fertilizer**.

HORROR FROM THE SKY

The Moores always planted a big garden. They planted potatoes, corn, peas, beans, and cucumbers. There were also tomatoes, spinach, squash, lettuce, radishes, cabbage, and onions. Taking care of the garden was a lot of work. But Calvin had to admit everything was awfully good—except the spinach.

The family had berries, grapes, and fruit trees too. Mom was really busy in the fall canning vegetables and fruits. Calvin, Margie, and George had to help.

By noon, Calvin had the chicken coop and the rabbit hutches cleaned. He was hot and tired when he finally went back to the house for lunch.

Chapter 2

Mom had made lemonade. Calvin drank a whole glassful without stopping. Then he drank another glassful and ate two sandwiches. He topped that off with two doughnuts Margie had brought home yesterday.

HORROR FROM THE SKY

Calvin yawned and stretched—a little more than necessary. But it didn't go over with Mom.

"I know you're tired," she said. "But there are things that have to be done. I'm tired too. I've been scrubbing floors and ironing all morning."

Calvin knew Mom and Dad worked hard. And now Margie and George were working hard. He realized he shouldn't be complaining so much.

But Calvin had been looking forward to summer vacation. Now all he did was work—all by himself.

"I wish we lived in town," Calvin said. "Then we wouldn't have so much to do. Ned lives in town. He doesn't have to work all the time."

"Maybe not," Mom said. "But his family has to buy their milk and eggs at the grocery store. And you know how Ned loves to come to our house. He loves the fresh fruit and vegetables we raise."

HORROR FROM THE SKY

Mom was right, as usual. Ned even liked their goat milk. Some of Calvin's friends wouldn't drink it.

The Moore family lived just outside the **city limits**. They wouldn't be able to have goats, pigs, or chickens if they lived in town. They wouldn't have room for such a big garden.

Calvin would have to walk to school. Now he, Margie, and George rode the school bus.

"It's too hot to work in the garden this afternoon, Mom," Calvin said. "Why can't I do it early in the morning? I did get the chicken coop and the rabbit hutches cleaned out."

Mom gave in. "Okay. But if you're going to be in the house, you can practice your piano lesson."

"But, Mom—" Calvin started.

"No arguments," Mom said. " I want you to spend at least an hour practicing."

HORROR FROM THE SKY

Calvin groaned all the way into the living room. Mom insisted that all of her children learn to play the piano. George had been allowed to stop piano and take trumpet lessons. He played in the high school band. Margie loved playing the piano. Calvin didn't mind it sometimes. But today he was not in the mood. It was too hot and **sultry**.

Calvin sighed. He sat down at the piano. He ran through the scales a couple of times.

All at once, Calvin remembered something. It was something Dad had said at the supper table the night before.

Dad had just finished a baked potato and two pork chops and swallowed the last of his coffee. Then he made his announcement. To Mom he said, "Helen, fix a quick and simple supper tomorrow."

Then to everyone he said, "Don't make any plans for tomorrow night. I'm bringing home a surprise."

"What?" Margie squealed.

"What kind of surprise would it be if I told?" Dad laughed.

"Give us a hint," Calvin begged.

Dad shook his head.

George looked interested, but he didn't say anything.

"Just a tiny little hint," Margie begged.

Dad thought for a minute. "Mmm," he said. "What's a good clue? Well—it's something we've never had before."

"That could be a lot of things," George said.

Dad got up from the table. He went into the living room. He started reading the newspaper. Everyone knew not to bother Mr. Moore when he was reading the paper.

"I hope he's not spending a lot of

money on something foolish," Mom murmured in a low voice.

Dad had done that more than once. He loved to buy **gadgets**. One time, he bought an automatic ice cream maker. The ice cream ended up looking like cottage cheese.

Calvin was so busy that morning he had forgotten about the surprise.

Calvin practiced the piano for nearly an hour. He practiced until his fingers started hurting.

Finally, Mom told him he could stop. She handed him a basket. "Please pick enough green peas for supper," she told him. "Then **shell** them."

Calvin filled the basket with peas. He ate nearly as many as he put in the basket.

After he finished shelling the peas, Mom handed him another basket. "Now pick enough strawberries for supper," she said.

Calvin mumbled as he picked the berries. "Now I'm doing Margie's chores as well as George's."

He ate more of the strawberries than he put in the basket too.

For the rest of the afternoon, Calvin sat in the porch swing reading. Calvin was just starting the third chapter of *Toby Tyler* when he heard Dad's car coming down the drive.

Calvin jumped off the porch. Even before Dad, Margie, and George got out of the car, he was shouting, "What's the surprise?"

George ruffled up his brother's hair. "That's what we'd like to know," he said "It's in the backseat. In that box."

"Dad picked it up on his lunch hour," Margie said. "He said we have to wait till after supper."

Even Mom pleaded with Dad all through supper. But Dad kept saying "Later."

HORROR FROM THE SKY

At last, "later" came. Supper was over, the dishes were done, and all the animals were fed. George even helped.

Dad brought in the box. He set it on the kitchen table. They all held their breath as Dad opened the box.

Chapter 3

It was a radio!

Dad was right. It *was* something they had never had before. Calvin had never even seen one before. He had seen pictures in magazines, but that was all. None of his friends had a radio.

Mom didn't complain this time. She didn't even ask how much it cost.

"Oh, Bert, how wonderful," she said. "I've wanted a radio for a long time. But I thought they were too expensive."

"Not anymore," Dad said. "They've come down in price. This one was on sale."

"Hurry! Turn it on, Dad," Margie begged.

"Slow down," Mr. Moore said. "We have to find a place to plug it in. And we have to hook up an aerial."

"An aerial?" Margie said. "What's that?"

"It's a wire that hooks to a screw on the back of the radio," George said. "Without an aerial, there will be no **reception**. Only **static**."

"Helen," Dad said. "Find a good place to put the radio."

HORROR FROM THE SKY

Mom cleared pictures and a lamp from a small table in front of a window.

"That's a good place," Dad said.

He opened the window.

"Go outside, George, and I'll hand you the wire," Dad said. "Hook it to the water pipe. That's supposed to give good reception."

Mom, Margie, and Calvin stood very still. They could hardly wait.

When George came back in, Dad turned on the radio. There was a click. Then a loud blast of static filled the room.

"Oh, Bert!" Mom cried. "It doesn't work."

Dad turned another knob. A voice came from the radio. It was a man's voice. The man was giving prices of hogs, beef, and chickens.

"What is that?" Margie whined. "I thought it would be music."

Dad laughed. "It won't be music all

the time. That's the farm price report."

Calvin couldn't believe it. They had a radio. He could hardly wait to tell Ned.

Dad turned the knob to another number on the dial. There was a lot of static. Dad turned the knob until the static was gone. A man's voice told them they were listening to station WTAM in Cleveland. Then the music began.

"Oh, good!" Margie cried.

She tapped her foot in time with the music. She began to sing along to the song. "Toot, toot, Tootsie, good-bye," she sang. "Toot, toot, Tootsie, don't cry."

Calvin groaned. "Oh, no."

Dad laughed. He began to hum along with Margie.

The station played some more music. Margie sang along with all the songs. George whistled along with a silly song about Barney Google, with his "goo, goo, googly eyes."

HORROR FROM THE SKY

After the music program, there was some news. Most of it was about President Coolidge. He was running for reelection.

The family stayed up late listening to the new radio. Finally, Dad said, "George, we'd better get to bed. We have to work tomorrow, remember."

The plant ran until noon on Saturdays.

"Don't forget the picnic tomorrow afternoon," Calvin reminded his father and brother.

"Forget fried chicken and potato salad!" Dad exclaimed. "Never!"

"And chocolate cake," Calvin said.

"I have tomorrow off," Margie said. "So guess who will probably end up making the cake."

Mom smiled and nodded her head.

"Be sure to take your fishing pole, George," Calvin said. "We'll catch a mess of fish."

George didn't answer.

"Okay?" Calvin said.

"Well—I—I," George stammered. "I—I may not be going."

"Not going on the picnic!" Calvin cried.

"I—I have plans," George said. "I'm going someplace. With—with some friends. We're going to have lunch downtown. Then we're going to a movie at the State Theater."

Dad said, "I almost forgot. I gave him permission." He looked at Mom. "I thought it would be all right with you."

Mom nodded her head.

"I bet I know who he's taking to the movie and lunch," Margie said teasingly.

George's face turned red. "Never mind," he mumbled.

But Margie didn't stop. "He's taking Betty Lou Martin," she said.

"Her brother, Art, is going too," George added.

"I'll bet he's taking Elsie Rull," Margie said.

"There's nothing wrong with that," Dad said.

George was still embarrassed.

Calvin just stared at his brother. George was going out with a girl! He was taking a girl to a movie instead of going fishing! Calvin couldn't believe it.

Dad turned off the radio, and the family went to bed.

Chapter 4

Calvin had a hard time falling asleep. He had been so excited about the family going on a picnic. It didn't sound as much fun anymore. Even having a new radio wasn't as exciting now.

HORROR FROM THE SKY

It wasn't enough that he had to do all the chores alone. It wasn't enough that his brother had a job and was gone all the time. Now his brother had a girlfriend.

George snored in the bed next to Calvin.

Boy, Calvin thought, I wish I was 16. I could have a job and make lots of money. I could go to movies. But I sure wouldn't take a girl!

And I'd buy a new bike, he thought. I wouldn't need George's old one.

It was late when Calvin finally fell asleep. When he woke, Dad and George were gone. Mom was frying chicken. Margie was mixing a chocolate cake. It was so hot in the kitchen.

"Hurry up with your chores, Calvin," Mom said. "Those goats have been bleating for an hour."

Calvin splashed water on his face at the sink.

HORROR FROM THE SKY

"I'm not very hungry," he said. "I'll just drink a glass of milk." He quickly swallowed the milk and went out the door.

A bucket of food for Nellie the pig sat on the back porch. The bucket was full of potato peelings, oatmeal from breakfast, sour milk, and other food scraps.

Calvin carried the bucket to the pigpen. Nellie snorted and grunted as she tried to climb over the fence.

"Be patient," Calvin grumbled. "You're not going to starve."

Calvin dumped the food into the **trough**. Nellie snuffled as she ate.

Next Calvin fed the chickens. He filled their water dish.

As he put feed in the goats' trough, they chewed on his shirt. "Stop it!" he grumbled.

They bleated and continued chewing on his shirt. But as soon as they saw the feed, they stopped. Then they spent more time butting heads than eating.

HORROR FROM THE SKY

Calvin thought about all the fun he and George had always had feeding and playing with the goats.

Calvin went to the rabbit hutches. He gave them food and water. He noticed something in Brownie's hutch. She had a new litter of baby rabbits. They were squirming under a cover of brown fur. Calvin uncovered the nest. There were seven babies. They were pink and naked.

Brownie was upset. She stamped her foot.

"Okay, okay," Calvin murmured. "I'm not going to hurt your babies." He replaced the fur.

Brownie was George's rabbit. George would be disappointed that he hadn't seen the **litter** first.

Serves him right, thought Calvin.

Calvin finished the chores and went to the house. Margie was frosting the cake. Mom was making potato salad. The kitchen smelled so good.

HORROR FROM THE SKY

"I'm going to weed the garden now," said Calvin.

"Good," Mom replied. "But you better call Ned first. Tell him we'll pick him up about one o'clock."

Ned was excited about going on the picnic.

"Don't forget to bring your fishing pole," Calvin reminded his friend.

Calvin spent nearly two hours working in the garden. He hoed two rows of corn and two rows of peas. He pulled weeds in the tomato patch.

When Calvin walked into the kitchen, the phone was ringing. His mom went to answer it.

Calvin went down to the basement to get his fishing pole. He also got Dad's pole and the **tackle box**.

Calvin climbed the stairs to the kitchen. The look on Mom's face told Calvin something was wrong. And Margie looked as if she could cry.

HORROR FROM THE SKY

"What happened?" Calvin asked.

"Dad has to work this afternoon," Mom said. "The plant has a special order to fill."

Calvin slumped down on a chair. He felt like crying too.

After a while, Mom put her hand on his shoulder. "I feel bad too," she said. "But next Friday is Independence Day. We can have a picnic then. After the parade."

Calvin sighed. "I'll call Ned," he said. "I'll tell him the picnic is off."

Ned was as disappointed as Calvin was.

"Well, at least I won't have to cook supper tonight," Mom said. "It's unusually hot and stuffy today."

"Look how cloudy it's getting," Margie said. "And it's so dark."

"Can I listen to the radio?" Calvin asked.

HORROR FROM THE SKY

"If you can stand to be in this hot house," Mom replied. "I'm going to sit on the porch and read my new magazine."

Margie followed Calvin into the living room. "I hope there's a good music program on," she said.

Calvin hoped there wasn't. But he didn't say so. He wasn't in the mood to listen to music.

Something called *The Children's Corner* was on. A woman was telling an Indian legend. It was a pretty good story. But right at the most exciting part, the **signal** faded away.

"What happened?" said Margie.

Calvin turned the knob a little. But there was nothing but static.

Rain began to hit the window.

"It must be going to storm," Calvin said. "Maybe a radio doesn't work in a storm."

HORROR FROM THE SKY

He turned it off.

What a dull, disappointing day,
Calvin thought. He went into his
bedroom. He stretched out on his bed.
In a few minutes, he was asleep.

Chapter 5

Calvin was awakened by the phone ringing. He rolled over on his bed, sat up, and rubbed his eyes. It was so hot. His shirt was stuck to his body.

The phone rang and rang. Isn't anyone going to answer it? Calvin wondered.

Calvin staggered to his feet. He made his way to the kitchen where the phone was. He saw Margie in the living room. She was asleep on the couch.

Calvin lifted the receiver. "Hello," he said.

"It's me," Ned answered. "Mom said I could have you spend the night. Can you?"

Calvin perked up at once.

That would be great. It was only a couple of miles to town. He could borrow George's bike. He didn't think George would care.

Calvin found Mom. She was asleep in her chair on the front porch. Her magazine was on the floor.

Mom didn't like the idea. "It's too hot to ride a bike that far," she said. "You could have a heatstroke. Besides it's raining."

Calvin argued, "It's stopped. See?"

"It's going to rain again," Mom said. "Just look at the sky."

Calvin looked toward the lake. The sky was very black. And it had a strange greenish tint. He had never seen the sky look like that.

"Please, Mom," he begged. "I'll pedal slow. I won't get overheated. I promise."

It took a lot more begging. But finally Calvin's mom gave in.

Calvin tied a string around a change of clothes. He added a towel and his bathing suit. Maybe they could go swimming at the lake.

He **doused** his head and face with cold water. It cooled him down a little.

Calvin wheeled George's bike out of the shed. He put his bundle in the basket. By the end of summer, Calvin thought, this will be my bike.

HORROR FROM THE SKY

He thought about George as he pedaled along. Dad had said George was getting off work early. He and his friends were going to the **matinee** at the State Theater. George would be with that girl. That Betty Lou Martin.

Calvin pedaled faster just thinking about it.

It began to rain again. It came down a little harder. The sky got even darker. Calvin saw streaks of lightning in the distance. The greenish tinge in the sky was **eerie**.

By the time he got to the edge of town, the rain stopped. The wind blew harder. That made it difficult to pedal the bike. Even though the wind was blowing, the air was still hot and sultry.

Sweat ran down Calvin's back. His eyes burned from the heat and the wind.

It became harder and harder to

pedal the bike. His legs were aching.

The rain started again. The lightning was getting closer.

It was all Calvin could do to stay on the bike. The wind whipped it one way, then the other.

Calvin looked ahead at the road. It was hard to see through the pouring rain. He thought he was very close to Ned's house.

A sudden gust of wind blew Calvin and the bike over. Calvin landed on the gravel. He skinned his arm badly. He got back on the bike. But again, he was blown to the ground.

He decided to walk and push the bike the rest of the way. He fought to hold the bike upright.

Suddenly, the wind tore the bike from his hands. It was lifted into the air. Calvin couldn't believe what he was seeing. The bike was sailing across a field.

HORROR FROM THE SKY

Calvin struggled against the wind. Lightning was all around him. The roaring of the wind was so loud he couldn't hear the thunder. Calvin could feel his heart pounding in his throat. He had never been so frightened in his life.

Over and over again, he was blown to the ground. A dark shadow passed overhead. Calvin looked up. It was a wooden wheelbarrow. It landed a few feet from where Calvin lay.

Finally, Calvin could no longer get to his feet. He tried calling for help. But he could not even hear his own voice.

All at once, he felt himself lifted into the air. "Oh, no." His cry was just a whisper. "Please, please, no."

But then, he heard a voice in his ear. It sounded miles away. "It's all right, Calvin," the voice said. "It's all right."

It was Mr. Heinz, Ned's father. Mr. Heinz held Calvin tightly in his arms.

He struggled frantically against the powerful wind. Calvin could feel his heart beating loudly in his ears.

After what seemed like hours, they reached Ned's house. Someone inside opened the door. It was Mrs. Heinz. "In the basement," she panted. "In the basement, quick!"

A moment later, Calvin was dropped on a mattress on the basement floor.

"Calvin, are you all right? It's me."

Calvin looked up at Ned. He tried to answer. But nothing came out. He lay still, gasping for breath. His whole body throbbed.

Overhead was the sound of timber splintering. The floor over the basement was jarred when a large tree fell on the house. Above the roaring of the storm, Calvin heard glass breaking.

Mr. and Mrs. Heinz sat huddled side by side. Ned sat next to Calvin on the mattress.

HORROR FROM THE SKY

It seemed that the roaring and crashing would never stop. But it did—as suddenly as it had started.

Calvin opened his eyes. He sat up. His shirt was ripped to shreds. His arm was bloody and sore.

"What—what happened, Dad?" Ned stammered.

"A tornado, I think," answered Mr. Heinz. "A very strange tornado. It seemed to go in all directions at once."

Very slowly, they all climbed the stairs. Mrs. Heinz burst into tears. Part of the roof was gone. Branches of a maple tree were in the kitchen. Dishes were shattered. All the windows were broken out. Furniture was broken.

Mrs. Heinz sobbed harder.

Mr. Heinz put his arms around her. "There now, Mama," he whispered. "We're safe. You, me, and our boy. We're safe." He smiled at Calvin. "And our good friend is safe too."

Calvin and Ned helped clean up what they could. They found two chairs that were not broken.

"Sit down, Mama," said Ned.

Mr. Heinz said, "I'm going out to see what damage was done around the town. I'll be back soon."

Chapter 6

Mr. Heinz came back an hour later. He looked very sad. He sat down on a chair next to Mrs. Heinz. Ned and Calvin sat on the floor.

HORROR FROM THE SKY

Mr. Heinz put his head in his hands. "You wouldn't know our town," he said with a sob. "There isn't a building that hasn't been damaged. Eight churches are destroyed." He stopped.

Mr. Heinz blew his nose and wiped his eyes. "I talked with a police officer," he went on. "He said many people have been killed. The tornado hit the **bathhouse** on the beach. There were people in it. It killed some." He took a deep breath. "The State Theater collapsed on the people inside. Many are dead. Some were only children."

Calvin jumped to his feet. "George!" he screamed. "George!"

Before anyone could stop him, Calvin ran from the house. The sight before him took his breath away. Cars were upside down. Houses were ripped apart.

HORROR FROM THE SKY

Calvin stumbled along the street.
Everywhere people were crying. They
were calling the names of loved ones.
He passed a dead dog crushed under
a power pole. Calvin's stomach
lurched.

Calvin walked on in a daze. He kept
thinking about what Mr. Heinz had
said. People had been killed in the
theater. His brother had been there.
Was he dead?

And what about Dad? Was Dad all
right? The Steel Stamping Company
was on the edge of town, far from the
downtown district. Did the tornado hit
there?

Calvin had no idea how far he had
walked. Nothing looked the same. He
hardly recognized the town.

Screams echoed in his ears. Babies
cried. Dogs barked.

Men dug through the **rubble**. Many
of them were in uniform. They were

firefighters, police officers, and soldiers.

Calvin saw two men uncover an old woman's body from a pile of splintered boards and bricks. They carried her past Calvin. He couldn't keep from staring. It was the first time he had ever seen a dead person.

At last, Calvin reached the State Theater. He nearly passed out as he looked around. His legs buckled under him.

The theater was mostly a pile of rubble. The beautiful balconies had crumbled into heaps.

"George! George!" he yelled. "George, where are you?"

Tears streamed down Calvin's cheeks. He ran toward the pile of **debris**, crying.

A police officer grabbed his arm. "Get back from there, son," he said. "That's dangerous."

"My brother is in there," Calvin cried.

"A lot of the injured have been taken away," said the police officer. "We're still searching for—for the bodies."

Calvin choked and coughed.

"I have to find him," he whimpered. "He's my brother."

"Just a minute, son," the officer said. He called to another officer. "Sam," he said. "Take this young fellow over to Central High School. See if you can help him find his brother."

Calvin followed the young officer.

"Why are we going to the high school?" Calvin asked.

"The hospital is full," Sam said. "We're using the high school as an emergency hospital. The Red Cross and the Salvation Army are also setting up tents on the lawn. Thousands of people are homeless."

HORROR FROM THE SKY

How awful, Calvin thought, to be homeless. To have your house suddenly destroyed.

"Be careful of the wires," said the officer.

Wires were down everywhere. At one corner, they had to climb over bricks and other rubble.

Sam held Calvin's arm.

"That's a bad **gash** you have there," he said. "Someone will clean it up and wrap it."

Calvin had nearly forgotten about his injured arm. The blood had dried, and it didn't hurt anymore.

A little girl was crying in front of a big house. The roof had blown away.

"Where are your parents?" asked Sam.

"They're cleaning up our house," said the little girl. "It got broken from the wind."

She pointed to an uprooted tree leaning on the house. "Bootsie won't come down," she said. "Will you get her for me?"

A black and white kitten was hunched up on a limb. It was terrified. Sam reached for the kitten, but it was just out of reach.

The kitten began to cry. The little girl cried harder.

"I think I can get it," Calvin said. He pulled himself up on a limb.

"Be careful," the officer said. "That tree could twist or turn any minute."

Calvin could hear the house creaking under the weight of the tree. He inched up a little farther. The kitten was crying frantically. Calvin reached out his arm as far as he could. He grabbed the kitten by the **scruff** of its neck.

The officer took the kitten from Calvin. He handed it to the little girl. Calvin worked his way down the tree.

HORROR FROM THE SKY

The little girl hugged the kitten close. "Thank you," she said. "Thank you for saving Bootsie."

Sam smiled at Calvin.

They walked on. At last, they arrived at the high school. Lots of people were helping. Some were putting up tents. Others were carrying injured people into the building.

Calvin shuddered at the sounds. People were crying and groaning. Some were screaming with pain.

Calvin didn't want to look. It was so awful. But he had to find George. He had to.

Oh, please, please, he begged silently. Don't let my brother be dead.

Calvin walked beside Sam.

"Calvin," someone called.

Calvin looked around. A boy was sitting on the school steps. His arm was in a sling. Calvin saw that it was Billy Fraser, a boy in his class. Billy had a bruise on his cheek too.

"Billy!" Calvin cried. "What happened?"

"I was at the movie at the State Theater," Billy said. "The whole building fell in. It—it was so terrible." Billy paused a moment. He wiped his eyes with the back of his hand. "Martin Cobb was—was killed."

Martin was another boy from Calvin's class.

Calvin swallowed hard. Martin Cobb was dead! Martin was only 11 years old. The same age as Calvin.

"Have—have you seen my brother, George?" Calvin asked. He held his breath, waiting for the answer.

Billy shook his head. "I saw him go in the theater," he said. "He was with some other kids. But I didn't see him after it happened."

Just then, Billy's folks came. They threw their arms around him. His mother cried.

HORROR FROM THE SKY

Calvin turned and walked away.

Sam had wandered off. He was searching for George too.

Calvin looked all around. He saw several people he knew. He asked everyone if they had seen his brother. No one had.

Then suddenly, Calvin saw a man walking out of the school building. It was someone he knew—Dad!

Calvin ran through the crowd. "Dad! Dad!" he cried, sobbing and choking.

Dad swooped Calvin up in his arms. "What—what are you doing here?" he asked.

Calvin explained all that had happened. Dad led Calvin back into the building. He took him to where George was lying on a cot.

George's right leg was in a cast. He had bruises and cuts on his face. Calvin tried to speak, but his words stuck in his throat.

His brother was alive! George reached and squeezed Calvin's hand.

At last, Calvin asked, "Is—is Betty Lou all right? And the others?"

Dad answered. "They all have a few scrapes and bumps. But they are all right."

"George," Calvin said. "I took your bike without your permission. It—it got blown away by the storm."

George grinned. "Well," he said. "I guess that means I'll have to buy two new bikes. One for you and one for me."

Finally, Dad said it was time to leave.

George had to stay for a couple of days. The doctor wanted to be sure he was okay.

"We'd better get home," Dad said. "Your mother and sister need to know that we are all right."

"Yes," said George. He grinned again at Calvin. "And you've got chores to do, little brother. After all, you have to do something for letting my bike blow away. And to pay for a brand new one."

Calvin and Dad laughed as they started for home.

Afterword

Saturday, June 24, 1924, seemed to be the perfect summer day to plan a family picnic. But that afternoon, the heat and humidity became almost unbearable. Dark clouds gathered in the west, and storms threatened.

The Lorain tornado hit the town of Sandusky, Ohio, before it reached Lorain. It is about 30 miles west of Lorain.

Sandusky received about $2 million in damages. Eight people were killed and about 100 were injured.

The tornado blew six cars from the ferry dock into the bay. A boathouse where a yacht was stored blew into the bay too.

From Sandusky, the tornado moved out over Lake Erie. It traveled across Lake Erie for a distance of 25 miles.

About 25 minutes later, the tornado moved inland from the lake. It struck the Lorain Municipal Bathhouse in Lakeview Park. Eight people were killed at the bathhouse. Many more were injured.

The tornado then ripped a three-mile path through the business district of Lorain. The path was as wide as 4,000 feet in some areas.

Over 1,000 homes were destroyed. All 200 businesses in the town received damage.

The State Theater collapsed. Over 80 people were in the audience. Fifteen were killed, seven or eight of them teenagers. Many others were badly injured.

In Lorain, eight cars blew into the lake. Other cars were picked up and blown through the air like toys. Over 200 cars were buried under bricks and other rubble.

Over 60 freight train cars were scattered on both sides of the tracks. Some were carried 30 feet.

Thousands of trees were uprooted. Some were carried through the air by the winds.

Some eyewitnesses claimed there were actually two tornadoes. One went through the Lorain business district area, then turned west. It tore through a residential area. Then it went north to Lake Erie. It met another funnel approaching from the lake. The two storms may have merged. Together, they swept to the east side of Lorain and caused much more damage there.

The storm did about $13 million in damages.

Glossary

bathhouse   building with dressing rooms where people can change into swimming suits

city limits   legal boundaries of city

coop   small building for housing chickens

debris   remains of something that is destroyed

HORROR FROM THE SKY

douse   to throw water on

eerie   scary

fertilizer   substance used to make
                 soil healthy for growing
                 things

gadget   small mechanical or
                 electronic device

gash   large cut

hutch   pen for animals such as
                 rabbits

litter   offspring of one birth

matinee   afternoon show

HORROR FROM THE SKY

pastries   sweet baked goods

pullet   young hen

reception   receiving of a radio
broadcast

rubble   broken pieces of
destroyed buildings

scruff   back of the neck

setting   hatching eggs

shell   to remove the outer
pods

HORROR FROM THE SKY

signal   airwaves that carry a
                     sound or image to a
                     radio or television

static   noise produced in a
                     radio by natural or
                     human disturbances

sultry   very hot and humid

tackle box   container that holds
                     fishing bait, lures, and
                     hooks

trough   long shallow, often
                     V-shaped, container to
                     hold feed or water for
                     animals